# What will
# Alex Do?

written by
## Toya Abbatiello
illustrated by
## Gloria Gedeon

Will Alex play with Dad?

No, Dad is mowing the grass.

Will Alex play with Mom?

No, Mom is washing the dishes.

Will Alex play with his brother?

No, his brother is climbing
a tree.

Will Alex play with his sister?

No, his sister is taking a nap.

Will Alex play with
his dog?

No, his dog is eating a bone.

Will Alex play with Grandma?

No, Grandma is reading.

Alex can read with Grandma!